ASK ME
HOW I GOT
HERE

CHRISTINE HEPPERMANN

ASK ME
HOW I GOT
HERE

Greenwillow Books

An Imprint of HarperCollinsPublishers

Ask Me How I Got Here

The text of this book is set in Carre Noir Pro. Book design by Sylvie Le Floc'h

Library of Congress Cataloging-in-Publication Data is available.
ISBN 978-0-06-238795-0 (hardback)

16 17 18 19 20 PC/RRDH 10 9 8 7 6 5 4 3 2 1
First Edition

Greenwillow Books

For Eric,

who doesn't have to ask

ASK ME
HOW I GOT
HERE

APRIL

Public School Kids Always Ask

How do you meet guys
if you go to an all-girls school?

Immaculate Heart Academy
is named for the pure love of God
that flows through Mary's heart.
But here's the *real* reason why
our logo is a hunk of dripping muscle:
five hundred girls in red plaid skirts.

Even if we brushed with garlic toothpaste
we couldn't keep the vampires away.

Not That All of Them Are Monsters

Sophomore year and I'm dating a junior
from our brother school, St. Luke's.
Craig is cute but kind of a jerk,
always getting too drunk.
Kissing him is like licking
the inside of a keg.

Nick is Craig's best friend.

He waits with me at Josie Hemple's party
while Craig pees in the bushes.

He lets me wear his sweatshirt
after Craig soaks me in Old Milwaukee.

Later he sits with me in Craig's car at Lake Calhoun
where the hockey team has decided
only pussies think it's too cold to swim.

He tells me Craig's a really great guy
when he isn't shit-faced.

We watch Craig whoop it up
in soggy boxer briefs,

and suddenly we both want
not to see that anymore,

so we slouch down in the seat,
and while we're there

a kiss just seems
to happen

which makes us sit up
straight
fast.

If We Tell Him

We should wait
until he sobers up.

Nick agrees. "Might be a good idea
for him to be conscious first."

God, those dimples are sweet.

He drives with one hand
on the steering wheel,
takes his other hand off my thigh
to turn down the heat Craig blasted
before he passed out.

In my driveway,
it's like we're the parents,
and Craig is our big drooly baby
asleep in the backseat.

"Think he's going to be pissed?"

"More like relieved."

"What?"

"Look, Addie, try not to be
too mad, okay? He's been
feeling super guilty.
He didn't know how to tell you
about him and Iris."

I Take It Back

All of them are monsters.

But Dammit

This one is adorable
as he presses his warm
forehead into mine,
wraps me in his
delicious demon breath,
whispers, "I'm sorry
Craig has been such a dick.
You deserve better."
I whisper back, "No kidding.
So give it to me."

"Right now?" he teases. "What if
Craig wakes up?"

"Then he gets one last look
at what he'll be missing."

Night Light

An hour later,
brushing my teeth,
I'm still glowing
in the dark.

MAY

First Love

It's hot.
It's sweaty.
It hurts so much.

I tune out my brain,
push through the pain,
until every part of me
craves it.

I want this feeling
to last forever
or at least for
another mile,
so I readjust
my earbuds and keep
running.

You Sure?

Sure I'm sure.

You're not doing this just because Craig said I'd kick your
   ass?

*Addie, there is no way you will kick my ass. And Craig can
   kiss it.*

Iris won't give his lips the time off.

*We should both be thankful that his lips have a constructive
   new hobby.*

I think you should wait for me over by the fountain.

Now I'm insulted.

Says the guy who hasn't run since eighth grade.

I've been conserving my strength.

Right.

Look, we're not climbing Mount Everest.

We're going up and down a dinky hill at the park a few times.

Ten times. Ten.

Numbers don't scare me.

Okay then, Mr. Mathlete. Run hard to the top. Coast to the
   bottom.

Got it.

You can stop anytime.

In your dreams!

You Sure? Part II

Nick?
. . . .
Don't just nod. Speak.
I . . . think . . .
Try to add a word next time.
I . . . think . . . I . . .
Good job! Another word?
willwaitforyoubythefountain.

Practice

Nick teaches bass at his uncle's music store.
I like to hang out there and wait for him.
Yesterday I was sitting at the back of the lesson room,
sort of studying for my biology final, sort of
staring into space while he worked with a squirmy kid
whose fingernails kept snagging on the strings.

Finally Nick said, "Let's give you a manicure, dude."
He opened up the scissors on his pocketknife,
and the kid sat completely still
while Nick trimmed each little nail.

And then they jammed.

It's No Wonder

the band Nick plays in is called Side Effects
because ingesting Milo's songs
has been known to cause nausea, eye rolling,
and an aversion to circuses.

Milo's never been a future Grammy winner,
but everything he wrote didn't used to be about
evil trapeze artists ("High Wire Murder-Suicide")
or evil Disney princesses ("Satanic Jasmine")
or evil hermit crabs ("Crustacean Femme Fatale").
Then Sabrina dumped him for Drake,
the inspiration for that Milo Christmas classic
"Die, Flaming Asswipe, Die."

End-of-School Bash

"What do you think?" I shout at Claire.

"What do I what?"
She signals for me to follow her
away from the speakers,

but I stay

while Milo writhes,
dry humps the mic;

while Jordan smirks, winks,
and juggles his sticks;

while Craig sinks to his knees
at the edge of the stage for a solo,
thrusting his crotch toward
the unlucky ladies in the front row;

while Nick stands with his head
bowed over his bass, startled
to find when he opens his eyes
that the world is still here.

After Party at Jordan's

When I say I feel like
a groupie,
a total cliché,
Nick reassures me: "You're not.
The bass player never gets
any action."

"So that's what I am"—besides
naked and ready
to dive under the bed
every time some dumbass drunk
jiggles the locked doorknob, falsettos
Hello? Anybody home?—"I'm
action."

"Who asked you
to move? Let me do all the work."

He scoots down by my feet,
gently parts my legs,
puts his face, his lips, his tongue
where Craig never would,
and wow
I'm so thankful
that Nick is a sensitive artist,
a total cliché.

JUNE

Minnesota

Land of ten thousand lakes,
nine of them right here in Minneapolis,
one of them only a few blocks
from my house.

I jog down to meet Claire. We like to run
early when it's still cool,
and the path isn't clogged with
ice cream carts and double-wide strollers.

The first thing she says when she sees me?
"You look like shit."

Always tactful, that girl.

"Nick and I were at Milo's till two A.M.
babysitting Iris. She took too big a hit.
Thought her lungs were on fire."

"Where was Craig?"

"Playing Guitar Hero. Somehow
his slammin' rendition of 'Sweet Child o' Mine'
didn't help her chill."

"What an asshole."

Always right, that girl.

Halfway around, I feel the magic
start to rise, feel it spread
through my muscles.
So I barely slept.
So what.
Stride by stride, breath by breath,
I'm waking up.

Nonviral Video

Three
"Likes" for the hot new Side Effects single
"Sea World Seduction,"
and—what the hell—I'll make it

four
because who would have thought
there were so many awesome rhymes for
Shamu?

Mom's Policy on Boys in My Room

"If you're brave enough for mad passion
with your sweet innocent mother right downstairs,
go ahead."

It was the same for my brother James
when he lived at home, though his room
was a pit that put girls in the mood
to update their tetanus shots.

Bottom line is, my parents trust me.
And they really like Nick.

Dad: "He has a good head on his shoulders."
Mom: "He's so polite!"

It's true; in fact just now
Nick asked me politely
if he was being too loud,
and I said, "I'll shut the door."

Fooling Around

Nick leans against my
headboard. "How was that?"

"Fantastic."

"Better than the first one?"

"I liked them both."

"Okay, tell me what you think of this."

My eyes on
his hands,
his hands on
the bass,
my mind on
the poem
I was
fooling around with
in my notebook before
he asked me to listen.

Nick's Been After Me

to write lyrics
because wouldn't it be great
for Side Effects to have one
measly song that doesn't make him
want to crawl behind his amp?

I can't.

Sure you can.

I can't!

How is it different from writing a poem?

My poems are not for, like, the masses.

Do it for me, Addie. Please?

Promise not to make that pathetic face ever again, and
I'll try.

I Can't ~~e~~

I can't lose you.
I can't find you.
I can't love you.
I can't define you.
I can't change you.
I can't accept you.
I can't erase you.
I can't let you
~~bum a cigarette~~
~~pet my marmoset~~
~~join a string quartet~~ ~~

Oh God

I'm Milo.

No,

you can't see what I wrote.

Yes,

I'll keep trying.

Sunday Morning

Just because we aren't in church
doesn't mean we haven't found
a place to worship
in the stained-glass shadows
underneath the Little League bleachers.
His mouth a skittish liturgy
along my neck,
my need a holy ache,
a blessing, I tilt back my head,
prepare to receive
communion.

A Risky Equation

Add one plus one plus
zero condoms to equal
pleasepleaseplease not three.

AUGUST

I'm Late

And Claire's already gone
around the lake twice—six miles—and can't stay
since she has to be at work at ten o'clock.

(Get this, she works at Claire's!
The one at Southdale. The same one
she used to shoplift sparkly shit
from in sixth grade.)

"Tomorrow?"
"Tomorrow. I swear."
"I don't know, Addie. Seems like
you're not giving one hundred percent."

She's channeling Coach so of course I can't
not flip her off as I dodge
a golden retriever and start my run,
promising myself I won't be late

again.

Nine Kinds of Late

It's-probably-nothing late.
Try-not-to-think-about-it late.
Cold-terror-in-the-middle-of-the-night late.
Oh-God-Jesus-no late.
Just-relax late.
It's-really-probably-nothing late.
Deep-breath late.
I-must-have-counted-wrong late.
But-what-if-I-didn't late.

That kind of late.

Then

Seventh grade. Religion class.
Sister Rose going on about
the stigmatics, women chosen by God
to bleed every Friday
at the hour of Christ's crucifixion.

It's supposed to be some
big honor, but to me it sounded like
a mess.

Now

I'd give anything
for blood
on this
bone-white pad.

Bodies

We raise them from babies.
They sleep every night in our beds,

so we tend to forget they're still wild.
Then one day they turn on us, snarling.

We're walking past a dark alley,
not paying attention. They pull us in,

push us down, cover our mouths
with hands we thought we knew.

Superstition

It means I'm not
if I step on every other stair,
if I turn the front doorknob with my elbow,
if the next four cars that drive by aren't black—okay,
green—
if I cross the street before the hand starts to flash,
if the poodle tied outside Walgreens doesn't bark,
if I walk down the "feminine care" aisle backward,
if the woman in front of me pays with cash—okay,
a credit card—
if I eat the receipt,
if I carry the bag home with my teeth,
if I light the vanilla candle in the bathroom,
if I hold the white stick in my left hand,
if I hold the rosary in my right hand,
if I make the sign of the cross ten times before I check
for
a minus
or

a plus.

Prayer While Flushing

Hail, Mary, full of grace,
You know what it's like
the Lord is with thee.
to wake up in a body no longer your own.
Blessed art thou among women
You take your fingers off the keys
and blessed is the fruit of thy womb,
but the piano keeps playing
Jesus.
until you become a song
Holy Mary, Mother of God,
you never knew the words to.
pray for us sinners
Who is with me, Mary?
now and at the hour of our death.
You?
Amen.

Drowning

Of course Nick won't leave me
when I tell him,
won't punch the wall or blurt
made-for-TV-movie lines like
How could you let this happen?
How do you know it's mine?

We're in my room.
He reaches up to pull me down
with him onto the beanbag chair.

He's my sturdy boat. My life raft.
Still, I'm sinking fast.
I open my mouth
and all that comes out
are bubbles.

The Good Boyfriend

drives me to Planned Parenthood,
rubs my shoulders in the waiting room,
holds my hand while the doctor with the horrible
coffee breath explains our options,
makes a stop at 7-Eleven on the way home,
buys a bag of Jolly Ranchers for us to share,
lets me have all the cherry ones,
tells me he can't stand that I have to go through this,
tells me he wishes like anything

he could take my place,

doesn't laugh when I call him
a typical guy, wanting all the fucking attention—*Nick,
I was joking!*—

drives the rest of the way to
his bad girlfriend's house
without saying a word.

After Nick Drops Me Off

I text Claire:

Worn out. Can't make it tomorrow.

SLACKER!!!

Sorry. I know.

Playing Mary

Third grade,
Claire and I lurching around her bedroom
holding our fake-aching backs.

Giving birth is easy—
reach under our T-shirts,
grab fistfuls of pillow,
and yank!

When we get bored with
Jesus and Jesus,
we put them down for a nap
in front of the TV.

Such good babies.
They never cry
when we sit on them
to watch cartoons.

My Purple Sauconys

I've been saving them for races.
They still have that new-shoe perfume.
If I rub the tread like a magic lamp,
can it zap me back to that big sale
at The Extra Mile when I first tried
these beauties on, bounced a few times
in front of the mirror, and knew
we were perfect together?

I shove the shoebox back
under my bed, try to concentrate on
the list of clinics.

It Is a Woman's Right

They will make me sign a paper
that says a licensed physician
has informed me of the risks,
has pointed out everything
that might perforate, tear, or
inflame.

Nick?
Oh, they'll give him
all the gory details,
too. If he wants. Or not.
Whichever. It's totally
up to him.

Unhappily Ever After

Once upon a time
a girl walked into the kitchen
to find her mother seated at the table,
drinking.

"Rough crowd at preschool story time?" the girl asked.

"How can you tell?"

"I'm psychic," said the girl, pointing
to the bottle of Absolut Raspberri vodka on the counter.

"Hyperactive little sugar fiends," said her mother,
aka Miss Emily, who, after more peaceful days
at the Elmwood Branch Library where she worked
as head children's librarian, limited herself to
Diet Fresca.

"Did they make you read *Zippy the Chipmunk*?"

"Yes," squeaked Miss Emily in her helium-overdose
rodent voice that hyperactive little sugar fiends love.

"Poor Mommy," said the girl, but she said it in a Zippy
squeak, too, and kept talking that way while Miss Emily,
laughing, plugged her ears and cried "Stop! Stop!
You're killing me!"

The girl liked to make her mother laugh.
She wished they could stay this way forever,
just two happy characters in a happy, funny story.
But they couldn't because, unfortunately,
Minnesota abortion law requires
parental notification.

Pro-choice

Going home from work on the bus,
a woman sat next to a man who was
eating a falafel wrap. It smelled incredible,
so she asked him where he got it.

That's why I exist:

Because my mother chose not to stand.

Because my father was not
in the mood for sushi.

Tonight

I
will
tell
my parents
tonight.

Or maybe tomorrow.

Just the Dirty Parts

Eighth grade. Health class.

That diagram up on the screen.

It looked like some kind of orchid,

or maybe an antelope skull at sunset,

but this was not art history,

and that was not a Georgia O'Keeffe.

Sister Joan said to cut the snickering,

but what did she expect?

It wasn't even a whole person, it was

just the dirty parts.

Not Just the Dirty Parts

I made Nick promise

not to tell anyone else

because

when people look at me

I want them to see

all of me.

When My Brother Started College

he stopped going to church.
His faith had faded and shrunk
like an old shirt,
and he could hardly remember
back to when it still fit.

Dad said, "Even if you don't believe
in God, He believes in you."

James and I rolled our eyes
at the time, but now I find myself hoping
it's true, that God has enough faith
in me to let me
make my own choices.

What Choice Do I Have?

Fling myself out the window?
(The screen is jammed.)
Run off and join the Marines?
(I look bad in hats.)
Hope the Earth explodes in the next ten seconds?
(One Mississippi, Two Mississippi . . .
Damn.)

Okay, enough stalling.
They're your parents, not a firing squad.
You can do this, Addie.
You have *to do this*
now.

Saturday Afternoon Avalanche

Dad's hypnotized
by the Twins game.

Mom's lost
in her book.

I'm curled
on the couch
with the cat who stays
asleep in my lap even as

the truth comes loose,
starts to roll.

My Dad Can Fix Anything

Paper jams, clogged drains, fuzzy screens,
that disturbing clang in the engine.

He's the king of the quick trip to Home Depot,
a wizard at unplugging and plugging back in.

When I was little he could make the goblins
under my bed go away just by turning on the light.

Inside the walls of his hug, I feel a little more
solid.

It's okay, Addie. Everything will be all right.
If only I could forget how he flinched

when my words hit,
as if something close to him
had shattered.

The Rinse Cycle

Mom escapes to the basement.
The dryer runs forever
before she reappears,
wiping her puffy red eyes
with the backs of her hands.

"That new detergent,"
she says. "I must be allergic."

"I'm sorry," I say.

"Me, too," she says.

"Damn Tide Clean Breeze."

"Damn it to hell." She laughs and
bursts into tears.

Mercy

Nick comes over. My
parents go out, come home later
with mint chip ice cream.

Hail, Addie, Full of Grace

Think how history might be different
if Mary had said to the angel Gabriel,
"You want me to do WHAT???
Are you totally nuts????
I'm only thirteen!
My parents would kill me!!!!"

and Gabriel had answered,
"Sure, I understand. No sweat."
and moved on to the next girl.

Nerves

We haven't trained
in the cemetery for ages,
since the company that
owns it—Corpses "R" Us?—
called the school to complain.

Yet somehow I'm back here,
feet slapping the road,
on either side of me a blur
of gravestones and trees.

Feeling good, feeling strong
when an angel swoops down
and attacks me. I cover
my head with my arms, but

waking up

is the only escape
from those furious talons and wings.

Six A.M.

I feel the way I always feel
the morning of a big race:
exhausted
from running all night
through my dreams.

You Must Have a Uterus to Ride

We tell Nick's mom
we're off to Valley Fair
for one last summer blast.

She tells us to have fun.

In a way, the clinic isn't so different
from an amusement park.
Nick hates rides that spin and plunge
and drop his lungs into his socks.
He'll wait in line with me
for Steel Venom,
but then they strap me in

without him

and he waves and meets me
at the exit.

The Runner

Last fall, after we'd lost two meets
in a row, Coach made us run hills
behind the convent, loop after loop
of coasting to the bottom, then pushing hard
to the top.

I tightened up and collapsed in the Virgin Mary
statue's shade. Above his clipboard, Coach
frowned, tugged at his mustache, told me
to walk it off. But Mary considered me
gently,

like the nurse at the clinic
as she spreads my trembling legs a little wider
while the doctor turns on the machine.

Ride Home

Are you okay?
Are you *okay?*
I'm pretty okay.
I'm pretty okay,

           too.

Sure?
Sure.
Does
it hurt?

       It hurts

           a little.

Anything I can do?

       You can stop worrying, okay?

       Okay.
I'll be fine. I'm just tired.
Should I stay with you?
You should drop me off. Go to Milo's. Really. I'm fine.

       If you're sure . . .
Positive.

Mom Has to Work

But before she leaves,
she fixes my couch nest,
brings me my notebook,
my phone, the remote,
ginger ale and toast as if
I have a stomach bug.

Do I want her to close the blinds?
Grab me another pillow?
Just stay home?

She's gone when I pop up
from the rabbit hole of sleep
unsure of where I am
until the hum of the ceiling fan
and the cramps
remind me.

Guardian Angel

The cat walks across
me, lies down right where I most
need a heating pad.

The Photo on the Piano

It's me at Calhoun Beach
before the sun burned me,
before the lake messed with my hair,
just a few days before
I took the test
and found out for sure.

Now when I walk through
the living room,
I set the frame facedown
only to come back later
and there I am again—
upright,
ignorant,
smiling.

Coach Says

Last season doesn't matter.
Those losses to Northstar
and Mondale and St. Paul Prep?
Never happened.

Last week doesn't matter.
Your butt was planted at the beach,
and all that ran was your mascara.
Last day of vacation. Fine.

What matters is right now.
What matters is that you commit
right now to training as hard as you can
and then harder.

He gives the same speech every August.
at our first cross country practice,
the practice I'm missing today
because the doctor said I should
take it easy.

When I Start Going Nuts at Home

Nick takes me to Cinema Twelve.

At the front of the concession line
a little kid throws a fit—
"Nachos *and* gummi worms, Daddy!"
When the guy turns to drag
his screaming brat toward
Karate Camels 4: Alpaca's Revenge,
I realize that Daddy is
Coach.

Nick thinks it's no big deal.
"So what if he saw you?
Tell him you had a twelve-hour bug.
Tell him all that leaning over the toilet
really stretched out your quads.
Tell him the second you stopped puking
You went out and ran wind sprints."

Wanna know what happens
in the first thirty minutes of *Dead End*?
No clue.
But after a while my buttered popcorn
stops tasting like burnt sand.
I start to relax. What's done
is done, I can't change it now, so why
let it ruin my afternoon?

Let Coach assume I'm a slacker.
Let him assume I skipped practice
for no good reason
because that's the truth.
Oh sure, I had a reason,
but never in a million years
would he call it good.

Going to Confession

When I was little, my sins were little, too:
a tiny bundle of lies. Unkind thoughts
about my brother. Still, to me, they weighed
as much as boulders.

Every month at all-school confession,
I rolled them through that narrow door
to show the priest how wicked I'd been.

Once when my teacher wasn't looking
I stepped out of line, snuck to the back
of the chapel, and slipped in
with the lightweights who had already
confessed and been absolved.

As I plopped down onto the pew,
I imagined it tilting
upward like a seesaw,
sending my classmates at the other end
flying.

Cafeteria Catholic

That's what they call you
when you buy some of
the church's teachings,
but not the whole buffet.

Mom is telling me about
the time when she was nine
and her cranky old parish priest
made her take off her
Gemini necklace before mass.

She couldn't convince him
that it *wasn't* a false idol.
It *wasn't* a sin.
It was a *birthday present*.

"The Catholic Church is run by men,"
she says as she digs out her wallet
to pay for my birth control pills. "And men
make mistakes."

The Advantages of Being Mary

She never had to listen
to excuses from Joseph
about how he <u>meant</u>
to bring protection
but must have left it
in his other donkey cart.

No drugstore trip—
Angel Gabriel makes house calls!

No peeing on an olive branch,
wrapping it in three burlap sacks,
sneaking it into Mary Magdalene's trash.

That long blue robe,
perfect for hiding
unsightly lumps.

Instead of condemnation,
a heavenly chorus,
a gold star.

Like Riding a Bike

In his room,
on his bed,
we kiss
for a long time.
He touches me
softly,
like I'm brand-new
and he's scared
I might break.

Well, I won't.

I take his hand,
place it where I
need it to be.

Hold on, Nick.
Here we go.

SEPTEMBER

We Are

the Immaculate Heart Crusaders.

It's not a game, a match, a race—
it's a holy war.

Rumor has it that the school board
wants to change our name
to something less eleventh century.

But whoever we are
will give *someone*
the wrong impression:

Bulldogs? Bull dykes.
Ravens? Satanists.
Wildcats? Sluts
prowling the sidelines
at St. Luke's homecoming game.

I say we go with Transplant
or Attack
or Burn.
Or wait—what about
the Immaculate Heart Breakers?

Then our opponents would know
we are so over them.

Our First Meet

An easy win, right?
Lakeside's course is pretty flat.
They have that one decent runner
and then the usual pack
of slow-motion stoners.

Heading into the final stretch,
running right beside Claire,
my right foot lands on something
squishy
and sli-i-i-i-i-i-i-i-des
just a little
just enough
for Claire
    to pull ahead.

I speed up.
    The Lakeside runner passes me.
I

s
l
o
w

d
o
w
n

from a sprint
to a jog
to a trot.

By the time I reach
the finish line it's like
I'm out
for a leisurely stroll.

Claire Is Almost Apologetic

about winning. "I didn't know
you were hurt!"

I am?

Coach examines my ankle
for swelling, finds instead
the glop of rotten apple
stuck to the bottom of my shoe.

"Next time I'll watch out
for hazardous fruit." I can joke
because it's just one race,
just stupid bad luck,

right?

It's Just One More Race

I walk again

in the Southwest Invitational

and again

in the meet against St. Paul Prep.

"Don't worry," says Nick. "It's early

in the season. You'll turn it around."

I'm not worried.

I know I can turn it around.

But maybe I don't want to.

Nick Makes Cardboard Signs

for the meet against North Tech
because maybe my problem is I just need to be
pumped?

He won't show them to me beforehand.
"That way," he says, "you'll run faster. To find out
what I have to say."

As I'm chugging toward the first mammoth hill,
he flashes
STRAWBERRY WAFFLES AND PAIN

At the dreaded halfway point,
he hits me with
LYME DISEASE LOVE CAVE

For the final turn,
he's ready with my personal favorite,
HARPOON MY HEART
What do you know, Milo's lyrics are good
for something:

I'm still walking, but at least
I'm cracking up.

Coach's Office

smells like Mexican food and menthol.
Pretty sure his lunch was a burrito
soaked in BENGAY.

"I know it's hard to get out of a slump,
Addie. But we'll work through it."

He points to the motivational poster—
a tiny runner, a rain-slick road—
behind his desk. He makes me read
out loud:

"Some hit the wall. Some crush it."

Ouch.

I think I'll just leave
that poor wall alone, thanks.

OCTOBER

It's Spirit Week

Or as the student council flyer says,
SPIRIT WEEK!!!!!!!!!!!!!!!!!!!!!!!!!!!!!!!!!!

Today is Monday, Pajama Day,
on which dressing like we're clinically depressed
demonstrates pep!

I'm wearing
my uniform! Same as always!
Because this *is* what I wear to sleep!
Through world lit!
And chemistry!
And every other class
I'm taking this semester!

I'm *so* committed to the theme
I'm practically a cheerleader!
"Gimme an *s*!" "Gimme a *p*!" Gimme a
Zzzzzzzzzzzzzzzzzzzzzzzzzzzzz . . .

In Morality Class

Allison Finley goes off about
how she would *never* take birth control pills
because they kill egg cells, which is like
having an abortion every month.

"Biologically speaking,
that's not quite the way it works,"
says Sister Barbara.

But Allison knows.
Her dad's a doctor—a gastroenterologist,
but, hey, close enough!—
and we will never catch *her*
with sinful ovaries.

Sister Barbara changes the subject
to our mid-semester projects,
due a week from today.
By now we should all have our topics.
She hopes we picked issues
we're passionate about.

For me that means an essay on . . .
apathy?

"I'm doing Hope's Journey,"
Allison barks, and then waits,
like she's a trained seal, and I'm
supposed to toss her a fish.

Oh, all right. "So what's that?
A movie about a lost Saint Bernard?"

"It's a counseling program
that helps women
repent after killing their babies.
Helps them, like, deal
with their grief. You should
Google it."

Um, yeah, thanks,
but I'll pass.

Kind of Like Yogurt

comes in different flavors,
nuns come in different orders.

There are the Carmelites,
which sound like Weight Watchers' sundaes,

and those off-brand Dollar Store pastries,
the Poor Clares.

The Sisters of Nazareth—
didn't they open for Pierce the Veil?

Who knows how the Daughters of St. Francis
were conceived, since Frank seemed more into
bird-watching than girls.

Immaculate Heart Academy
was founded by the Servants of Our Blessed Mother.
They pride themselves on their compassion
for all who suffer.

Which is funny because last year
Sister Bridget had Liz Morley carry
a box of calculus textbooks
up three flights of stairs during detention.

Liz was six months pregnant.

If that's what the Servants of Mary
call compassion, wouldn't you hate
to see compassion at a school run by
the Handmaids of the Precious Blood?

Sister Barbara's Okay, Though

She also teaches
sewing, where Liz learned to make
maternity skirts.

A Head Start on the Homework or . . . Not

Dorothy Day worked tirelessly for social justice. In 1933, at the height of the Great Depression, she founded The Catholic Worker *newspaper to advocate for the poorest of the poor and, in her words, "for those who think that there is no hope for the future." What individual or social movement today gives you hope for the future? Explain why.*

~~The receptionist gave me hope for the future when she said your appointment's all set, we'll see you next Friday.~~

~~The nurse gave me hope for the future when she said the doctor is just finishing up with another patient, she'll be in shortly.~~

~~The doctor gave me hope for the future when she said you'll feel some discomfort but it will be over soon.~~

The Bell Rings

And I can't escape Claire.
I'm the helpless swimmer;
she's the shark
knifing through the hall
in a Hello Kitty robe,
pink slippers shuffling
straight to my locker.

"You're really not going to practice?"

"I am really not going to practice.
Because, if you remember back
to last Friday, I am really, really
kicked off the team."

"Technically? You quit."

"And wasn't it touching when
Coach begged me not to?
Oh wait, that didn't happen!"

"He'd take you back in a second.
Just cry in front of him. Men
can't handle tears."

"Claire, he's my coach, not
my boyfriend." *Shudder.*

"All I'm saying is it worked for me
in geometry. A little liquid and, boom,
Mr. Saltzman let me retake the final.
Didn't even have to reapply my eyeliner."

"I'll pass."

"Okay, let me do it for you." Claire
scrunches up her face. "Coach Gray,
Addie works her *butt* off
for this team. So she had a few off races.
So what? She's still our best runner.
We'll never make it to State
without her. And frankly?
I don't want to."

She wipes her eyes on her
fuzzy sleeve. Smiles. "Well?"

I do a slow clap. "Impressive,
Jennifer Lawrence."

"I'll march into his office
right now. Just say the word."

"Don't."

"A different word?"

"No."

She sighs. "Fine. Suit yourself.
And let me borrow your sports bra.
Mine hasn't been washed in forever.
It stinks."

The Weird Thing Is

Claire's not acting.
When she says she wants me back
on the team, she means it.

Clearly
I am a horrible friend
because
if I were in her place,
I'd never beg Coach to bring back
my biggest competition.

Last year she beat me
once,
but it didn't seem to give her
a rush. She hugged me
same as always and said,
"Good job," and I hugged her
back and said, "You, too,"
and I was the one
acting.

Nick Texts

Going to practice?
Yep
Me too. Milo has a new song
Not even going to ask
Remember "Hobo Love Hotel"?
Unfortunately
It's worse
Worse than "God Eats at Denny's"?
Worse than "Helen Keller Stare Down"
Poor you
If someone would just write a song for us . . .
I've been busy
I forgive you
Gee, thanks, Father Nick
Bless you, my child. Run fast.
Don't I always?

Why Drive All the Way to Java Joe's

when Caffeine-8 is only two blocks
from school?

At Java Joe's there's no Betsy
behind the counter. There's a
scruffy dude with a goatee,
his most probing question,
"Skim or two percent?"

At Java Joe's the woman
grading papers by the window
doesn't look up from her latte
and say, "Hey there, Addie. Did Coach
give you the day off?"

At Java Joe's the two girls
on the saggy flowered couch
can whisper all they want, and
I don't care. I don't know them;
they don't know me.

Stay or Go

I always order my coffee to go,
since I'm always running off to go
running, but now I have nowhere to go
for at least two hours!!!!! If I go
home now, Mom and Dad will know that I didn't go
to practice, and I can't imagine *that* going
well, the conversation in which I admit I have gone
and fucked up. Yet again. Why should I go
through the ick of confessing when I can go
on pretending I'm still on the team, when I can go
to this warm, lovely coffee shop instead of going
on to my parents, to Nick, about why I won't be going
to college on a cross country scholarship. (Sorry! My bad!) I go
over to a table near an outlet, dump my backpack, go
up to the counter, order a turtle mocha with whipped cream to
stay.

Two. Whole. Hours.

Just think what I can accomplish.
No more weights to lift.
No more miles to log.

That's right, I see myself telling
the reporter from *Runner's World.*
I quit cross country to focus on my studies.

Watch me fire up my laptop.
Watch me pick up the pace.
Watch me get shit done.

Cute or Cruel?: The Ethics of Feline Lederhosen

The only morality project

for which watching

twelve Kranky Katz videos

in a row

might possibly count

as research.

When the Holy Spirit Came upon Her ⌐

Mary must have felt

??
?????????? ⍦

The Girl Ordering a Soy Chai

looks like death
in her oversized black sweatshirt,
hood up Grim Reaper style,
and Abercrombie Cadaver Fit jeans.

Death extends a pale claw
to grab her change,
turns,
grins,
calls my name.

Death

is Juliana!

I haven't seen her in, what,
two years? Not since she graduated.

She pulls down the hood and transforms
again into a mutant version
of the Juliana I used to know. Her hair
was long and blond; now it's short and
seasick green.

But those eyes. Damn. They're still
so intensely blue. Like she dug them
out of a mine in Sri Lanka.
Look into those magic crystals
for long, and you get woozy.

"What are you doing here?" she asks.

"Windsurfing." I'm playing it cool,
sweeping my backpack off the other chair
so she can sit down.

"Emphasis on the *here*, smart-ass,
not the *what*. I'm *here* every day,
and I haven't noticed you before."

"Let's see." I pretend to think. "I'm *here* today because *there* has too strict a dress code?"

She laughs her same old laugh. I'd know it anywhere.

For the Record

When Coach wants to shame,
I mean, inspire us, he reminds us
of Juliana's senior year, when he
practically wrecked his knees
climbing up and down
and up and down
and up and down
that giant ladder in the gym
to change her time
on the record board
after every meet.

About as Long as It Takes

for her to shake
a packet of Splenda into her drink
is as long as I can wait
before blurting, "I'm hiding
out here because I quit
cross country."

She was going to ask
about the team eventually,
right?

Her pierced eyebrows
rise into her bangs. "You have to hide?
Coach is . . ." She leans close.
"hunting you down?"

"No. It's just . . . It's a long story.
A long stupid story." *Why
is she smiling like that?* "How's
cross country at the U?"

"I have no idea."

"What do you mean?"
Her mile-long legs stretch
alongside the table. "I'm not running,
either; I'm sitting this season out."

Juliana not running.
That's like a fish not swimming.
A bird deciding to stop flying
and start taking the bus.
It makes no sense, unless . . .

"So you're injured?"

"Give me a minute
to figure out how to answer that."
Her phone buzzes. She doesn't
pick it up. "I can't honestly say
I'm not uninjured."

"Oh God, let me guess. You're a philosophy major.
My brother is a philosophy major."

She grins. "Anthropology. But, really,
Addie. I'm taking some time off. It's
no big deal."

Don't You Have a Scholarship?

"Had," she corrects. "I *had* a scholarship."
Her phone interrupts—*Look at me!*
Look at me!—and this time she obeys.
"Hey, I've got to get going. Want to meet
here tomorrow? Same time?"

"Let me check my calendar." I
blink. "What do you know, no plans."

"Okay, then. To be continued."

"It's so crazy
that we ran into each other."

"Like I said, I'm here practically
every day." Her hood swallows
her face. "My shrink's office is
right around the corner."

Ugh

I cannot believe I said "crazy."

Then again . . .
she sees her shrink
Every. Day.

Maybe they just
like each other a lot!

They could be in the middle
of a time-consuming project:

A crocheted straight jacket!
A Xanax mosaic!
A production of *The Sound of Music*
starring Juliana as Maria,
and the rest of her
multiple personalities
as the von Trapps!

Stop It, Addie

You are not one to judge.

When the Holy Spirit Came upon Her

Mary must have felt

something—

a warmth or a chill,
a tingle in a strange place,
an ache that suddenly
made sense or no sense
at all, because how could she be
the one the Lord had chosen
as His magic hat?
Abracadabra, there was

something

inside her, and she had to explain
to Joseph, her parents, the neighbors
holding the stones that she did

nothing

but lie there and let it happen.

At Home

I drop my duffel
full of sweat-free sweats,
find Mom standing beside
the wide-open fridge.

"I'm a lettuce murderer,"
she confesses, showing me
the victim's putrid corpse.

"It died from neglect.
You're more of a
lettuce abuser."

"Thanks. Frozen
peas okay?"

"Sure. I'll nuke them."

"These chicken breasts."
She sniffs the package. "How long
have they been in here?"

The Complete Works of Shakespeare
she can handle, but with
expiration dates she's illiterate.

"Please, ma'am, put down the poultry
and back slowly away from the appliance."

"Here's an idea: You cook. I collapse in a heap."

"Rough day at the psych ward, I mean,
library?"

"Not too bad. No one dumped crayons
in the boys' toilet or asked me to help
print out naked pictures of Halle Berry.
I'd call that a win."

The questionable chicken
sizzles in the pan. I pour the peas
in a colander, wash away
incriminating freezer burn.

Speaking of Psych Wards . . .

"Remember Juliana?
I saw her this afternoon."

"Oh!" Mom's eyes brighten.
"How's she doing?"

"Pretty good. She was
running at the U, but she's
not anymore."

"Coach must have had
something to say about that."

"How would he know?"

"You said she stopped by practice."

Because that's where I was
this afternoon.

"She didn't tell him."

"Well, good for her. Nothing wrong with a break."

This is where I say it, right?
I'm so glad you feel that way, because . . .

"When's your next meet?"

"Um, Friday? In Bloomington?"

"Perfect. I'm off Friday."

"You don't have to come."

"Of course I'm coming, silly."

Crap!
The peas are exploding.
I hit Clear, pop open
the microwave.

Everyone help yourself
to a delicious bowl
of shrunken Martian heads.

Dad's Fix for the Peas

"Butter, garlic, and
voilà!" For the chicken:
"Not *burned*. Cajun style."

Dinner Conversation

Mom: "Have you noticed that things keep falling down?
The shelf in the bathroom. And stuff on top of the piano.
Addie, I must set that photo of you back up five times a day."

Me: "I blame earthquakes."

Dad: "I blame herds of wayward elephants.
Or wait, when do the bulls run in Spain?
Maybe this year they took a Minnesota detour."

Mom: "Ha-ha, very funny. Though I did just read
somewhere that earthquakes can be so slight
you don't even feel them."

Me: "And only dogs can hear them."

Dad: "And only worms can smell them."

Mom: "Now that *would* be a miracle of nature,
since worms don't have nostrils."

Me: [Laughs. Bites into a roll.]

I Feel More Like

a hurricane.
Hurricane Addie,
the unnatural disaster,
whirling through
the living room.
Where she touches
down?
So predictable.

Seven New Messages

Working till eight. Wanna stop by?

You can put together a drum set.

Or look at songbooks for INSPIRATION.

You okay?

Addie?

Helloooooooooooooooooooooooooooooo??????????????????????

Calling you.

The Trinity, Explained

It's supposed to be some big mystery,
how God can be three-in-one.
But don't all of us come in pieces?

I'm the daughter
who can't stop making bad choices;
the girlfriend
who won't answer her phone;
the ghost
who is anything
but holy,
no matter how hard she tries.

I Wait Until 9:15 to Call Nick Back

and say sorry, my phone was dead.

Crunching spicy peanuts, he complains
that his last two lessons cancelled. Then
he had to inventory violins "all alone. Sniff."

I tell him I would have been no fun because
"I'm exhausted. Coach worked us hard."

"That guy's a tool. He needs to go
easier on you."

"No, he doesn't. It was fine."

"I just think . . ." But Nick
has to quick find some ginger ale,
his mouth is on fire!

Possible Morality Project ✐

The Pros and Cons of Lying to My Boyfriend

Pros:

The truth is too complicated.

The truth requires confrontation.

The truth requires energy.

The truth would make him look at me
with worried walrus eyes.

The truth is more than I can handle right now.

The truth can wait.

Cons:

I will have to tell him the truth
eventually. ⚡

Protest

In the middle of the night,
no matter which way I turn,
my legs twitch like downed wires.

I try deep breaths. Counting
backward: 100, 99, 98,
97 ... At 65 they stop
and then start up again

more desperate than before,
begging the twisted sheet to
let them go,
they need to get out of here
fast!

Tuesday: Wacky Hair Day

On which no fauxhawk or rainbow Afro wig
can top Sister Carol's furry mole.

In French, I pat Claire's buns—
her fat round Princess Leia braids—
and say, "Why am I suddenly hungry
for cinnamon rolls?"

"Lay off my delicious locks, Solokowski.
At least *I* made an effort."

"I made an effort, see?" I display my
unshaven leg. "I'm Chewbacca!"

"Zip it, mademoiselles," says Monsieur Shapiro
as he hands back our last pop quiz
on *le symbolisme dans Le Petit Prince.*

Claire whispers, "Mira's shin is killing her.
Coach thinks it's a stress fracture. She's out for at least
two more meets. Maybe the rest of the season."

"Oh man, that sucks."
"That's all you can say?"

"I'll send her a get-well fruit basket?"

Princess Cinnabun shakes her wacky head, "Our team's falling apart, Addie, and you don't even care."

"I do too care. I'll toss in a balloon bouquet."

Quiz

Write a paragraph that incorporates ten or more words and phrases from the review list for chapters 1–6 of Le Petit Prince.

Une jeune fille a couru à travers <u>la forêt vierge.</u> Elle pensait qu'elle courait vers la maison, <u>mais elle se trompait.</u> Elle courait jusqu'à ce qu'elle soit <u>morte de fatigue.</u> Elle s'assît sur <u>une racine.</u> Il y avait des baies dans l'arbre, mais elle <u>mourait de faim.</u> Il y a un ruisseau, mais elle <u>mourait de soif.</u> Elle <u>éclata de rire.</u> <u>Un papillon</u> géant <u>l'a emporté.</u>

(A young girl ran through the untouched forest. She thought she was running toward home, but she was mistaken. She ran until she was dead tired. She sat down on a root. There were berries on the tree, but she was dying of hunger. There was a stream, but she was dying of thirst. She burst out laughing. A giant butterfly carried her away.)

Creative! But you only used nine vocabulary words. B-

Solitary Confinement

Our morality textbook covers
abortion and capital punishment
in the same chapter.

"Duh." Allison snorts. "They put
all the murderers together."

Sister Barbara asks, "Anyone see
a different connection?"

Allison leaps to her feet.
If this was once a discussion,
now it's a lecture. "So I've been
reading a lot of really sad stories
on the Hope's Journey website.
These women, they've had abortions,
and now they have nightmares.
They can't eat. They can't even *look* at
a baby or a pregnant woman without
wanting to die. So that's like
death row, right?"

"Guilt can be a prison," Sister Barbara agrees.
"No matter what we've done, God
always forgives us, but it can be hard
to forgive ourselves."

Above her head,
the clock glares like a guard
making sure I stay locked
in this airless cell
where every minute is
ten years to life.

It Takes Me Back

Hurrying past the picketers
on my way into the clinic,
I saw a girl
I thought was Allison—
tall, blond ponytail, beaky nose.

On my way out,
I lifted my head
to get a closer look,
and realized
I was wrong
and so was she:
not even Allison
would spell *murder*
with two *d*'s.

Annunciation at the Coffee Shop ✏

Mary speaks:

So about nine months ago I came in here and ordered a nonfat
caramel latte, and you know how sometimes the barista makes
a rad shape in the milk, like a heart or a flower or whatever?
Well, when I went to pick up my drink, sweartofuckinggod,
there was an angel in my coffee! The outline of wings and a
face and hair. And a staff or some kind of wand thingy. So I
go to the barista, that's amazing, how did you do that, and
she's all, do what? And I'm all, make an angel, and I showed
her my cup, and she stared down at it for a few seconds. Then
she said, Huh. My bad. I was trying to make a tree. Which is
proof, because she wasn't <u>trying</u>. The angel just appeared. I took
a pic with my phone, but it came out all blurry, which is even
more proof, because angels aren't supposed to show up on film
or in pixels or whatever. Or maybe that's vampires. Anyway, I
know I should have saved it, I could have made a ton of money
selling it as, like, some kind of healing potion, but I drank it
because I really fucking needed the caffeine. ⚡

No Offense

The scruffy barista nods at my skirt.
His sister went to Immaculate Heart.
Do I know her? Megan Snoratoscafitz
or something like that? I shake my head.

"She said it sucked there, no offense."

None taken, dude. I'll just put your tip
back in my wallet, no offense!

He tells me she transferred to Arbor Hills.

Yeah, I hear that's a good school
for scoring cheap cocaine.

Java Joe's Is Packed

To snag a table,
we vulture over a woman
apparently reading to her
empty coffee mug.

"You're so lucky," I tell Juliana
as we sit down. "Not to have to wear
a uniform anymore."

Today she's in dark green jeans,
a red Zombie Kids T-shirt.
Add the hair, and it's
Christmas in the mosh pit.

She shrugs. "I kind of miss it."

"You miss walking around looking like
a Catholic American Girl doll?"

"I miss not having to think."

"But since when is thinking a bad thing?"

Across from us, twins in identical onesies
gum blueberry muffins as their mother
communes with her laptop.

I'm on a roll. "I mean, uniforms are supposed
to make it so we're all the same, right?

Like we all don't know that Allison Finley
spent last summer in Florence,
and Heidi Demming's dad is the custodian."

"Hey, Mr. Demming is cool."

"I agree, but I'm pretty sure he doesn't
earn six figures refilling tampon dispensers."

"Let's cut back on the gesturing
if you're going to rant against injustice."
She takes my latte out of my hand. "I'm scared
you're going to get burned."

Well, What Do You Know

I'm ranting!
And it feels pretty good!
Maybe it's the caffeine
or the fact that
Juliana's eyes
are sosososososososososososo
crazy
hypnotic
Caribbean fucking Ocean
blue
that I can't seem to
shut up,
that when she suddenly
asks me
why I quit the team
I plunge right in
and tell her
almost—
almost!—
everything.

The Espresso Machine Makes Angry Dragon Noises

Juliana
snorts?

"You're laughing at me?"

"I'm laughing at *us*. At how pissed Coach would be
if he saw us sitting here. His former stars.
I used to care so much whether he thought
I was fulfilling my potential . . ."

"Believe me, he did."

"Well, so what? Who is he?
An old guy with a stopwatch and
a cheesy-ass mustache."

"He shaved it."

"He shaved the sex caterpillar?" she says
with enough decibels that the twins' mom
swivels. "Aw, now I'm kind of sad.
I may need a chocolate scone to ease my grief.
Want one?"

I say sure, but then watching her
stand in line, I realize I don't
need anything, really, because I'm—
what's the word?—oh yeah:
happy.

One Time After Practice

Juliana gave me a ride home.
She came in to hang out for a while.
James practically started drooling.
He sat close to her on the couch.
I squeezed in next to him.
We all watched *The Simpsons*.
I felt something tickling the back of my neck.
I screamed and jumped up.
She wiggled her fingers and said,

"The sex caterpillar is going to sting you!"

She chased me around the den.
We were laughing so hard,
we almost peed our pants.
Neither of us noticed James
get up and go in his room.

Screw Cross Country

"It's not as if we live in Panem and
the other tributes are chasing us
with crossbows. They should give medals
to whoever can identify the most wildflowers
or, like, collect the most beautiful leaves."

Juliana plucks a chocolate chip
the color of her nail polish, pops it
in her mouth.

"They do," I tell her. "It's called Girl Scouts."

"You've got to separate yourself
from the story."

"What story?"

"Spencer, my shrink, says that.
It means don't automatically assume
that you're the one who fucked up.
Why not blame Coach or your parents or . . ."
she flings out her arms, "the goddamn
high school athletic association
for twisting your priorities? You're not
a robot, Addie. You don't have to run
whenever they flip your switch."

The Story

"But I love running. Or
I used to."

Over by the window
a man shouts a language
I don't understand
into his phone.

"Yeah," she says. "Me, too."

A Runner's Guide

Some pain
you can run through.
Some pain
you can't.
You try to ignore it,
but it only gets worse.

You can't always tell
which kind you have.
It's best to play it safe
and stop
so you don't risk
serious injury.

No Excuses

Nick's text says I absolutely have to
stop by the store tonight. He's got
a surprise.

*Surprise, I'm adopted, and you're actually
my sister!*

Surprise, my teeth fell out!

Surprise, well, all but two! In the front!

Surprise, I'm going on tour with Michael Bublé!

Surprise, I meant Mr. Bubble!

Surprise, I'm joining the priesthood!

Surprise, I'm pregnant!

Only thing I know for sure is
it's not that.

Closing Time

Nick grabs a guitar
from the display above the counter,
leads me back to a practice room
so crammed with dusty songbook racks
there's barely space for two chairs.
Is he going to teach me some chords?
Just listen.
He's tuning, and it's taking forever.
Okay, he's ready now.

His playing's a little timid at first,
like a shy animal I don't want to scare
away, so I hold still while it grows
stronger, more sure of itself. This melody,
it might be Bright Eyes or Bon Iver.

But of course I know the composer. He's
right here.

Isn't It Romantic?

Turns out he wrote the song
for me.

"We'll need time to practice
it before the Halloween gig,
so how about if you give me
the lyrics next week?
Think you can finish by then?
What's wrong? Why are you
looking at me like that?"

Just Another Breakup Song

Male vocals: I can't believe you're mad.

Female vocals: I can't believe you didn't think I would be!

Male vocals: This is nuts. I did something to *help* you.

Female vocals: No, you did something to help yourself.
There's a difference.

[Guitar solo]

Male vocals: I'm not asking you to compose a rock opera.
It's one stupid song.

Female vocals: If stupid is what you're going for,
ask Milo.

Male vocals: Exactly.

Female vocals: I told you. I'm busy.

Male vocals: Right. All that training. It's really paying off.

Female vocals: You did not just say that.

[Drum solo]

Male vocals: Look, you could write decent lyrics
in, like, ten minutes. But for some reason you
won't.

Female vocals: I'm not your robot.

Male vocals: No, but you have to admit,
I'm pretty good at turning your knobs.

Female vocals: Don't try to joke your way out of this.

Male vocals: Excuse me for thinking that maybe
this one fucking time you'd do something nice for me.

Female vocals: Separate yourself from the story, Nick.

Male vocals: What's that supposed to mean?

Female vocals: I don't know. I just . . . I can't . . . I guess
I'm done.

The Drive Home: A Scattered Refrain

Fuck him.
Who does he think he is?
That asshole.
What's my problem?
I'm such a bitch.
I'm sorry.
I'm sorry?
What's my problem?
Fuck him.
Who does he think he is?
That asshole.
I'm sorry.
Not my problem.

Windy Night

Under the streetlamp,
yellow leaves swarm
like lost bees.
Do the trees feel
lighter without them?

Wednesday: Favorite Celebrity Day

Kara Howser wears a "Boy Crazy" T-shirt,
tells Sister Carol she's Miley Cyrus, but really?
She's Father Thom.

"Get it?" says Claire. She has a picture
of a compass pinned to her chest,
the red arrow pointing east. "I'm
One Direction. And look at you!"

It's not like I planned my costume.
More like this morning I stepped
out of the shower and wrapped myself in
the obvious.

Playing Mary II

On the square of rug
the dampness spreads
like miracle roses.
I drape the blue towel
over my head, wipe
the steam from the mirror, and
she appears.

Allison Gives Me a Hint

"I want to make out with myself."

Hmmm. Olive green thermal. Matching cargo pants.
"You're G.I. Joe?"

"You freak! I'm Liam Hemsworth!" She
fake pouts. Then, "I'm surprised they let you
wear that. It's sacrilege."

So says the girl dressed as
her own masturbatory fantasy.

"No it's not. It's a hundred percent cotton."

"Seriously, Addie. When I was in fourth grade?
This kid got sent home from school on Halloween
for dressing as Jesus. Mark Price. He kept
whacking me with his cross. What a jerk."

"Sounds like my son had a crush on you."

"Your son? Oh, right." Liam giggles and
coats his lips with tinted gloss. "He did look kind of cute
in that loincloth."

Celebrity Mom

Everywhere she sees him
hanging—
above altars, on the walls
of salons and service stations,
from chains around the necks
of pimply clerks who bag her bread
with melons, reminding her
to have a nice day.

She can never forget
the night he left with his friends,
how she made him promise
to get a haircut,
pushed his bangs away from
his beautiful eyes.

All Sister Barbara Says

when she sees me is,
"So I assume you didn't
just come from swim class."*

*Immaculate Heart
has a natatorium?
Ha! We're not Lakeside!

She Gives Us the Whole Hour

to work, so I get busy
on *Cathartic or Petty?*,
my highly personal quest
to turn all of the "Nick"s
in my notebook to "~~Nick~~"s.

Allison puts her head down
on her desk. Lifts it. Looks at me.
Sniffs.
I don't ask what's wrong;
she will tell me in 4, 3, 2 . . .

"These are just so sad, Addie.
You wouldn't believe it."

"Believe what?"

"These letters. Listen."

No need to ask if I have a choice.

She begins. "Dear Matthew,
I think about you every day.
I . . ."

"Wait. Stop. Who is Matthew?"

"Her baby. Hope's Journey
has women write letters to their
aborted babies. It helps
the healing process."

"Sounds morbid to me."

"No, it's part of the grieving ritual.
To give the baby a name
and ask him for forgiveness.
Though I guess she can't really
know for sure it was a boy.
I'd name it something unisex.
Like Devon. Or Jordan."

"How about Beelzebub?"

"That's not funny, Addie."

"Bub for short."

"Don't you take anything
seriously?"

"Not if I can help it."

Dear ?????????????????????????? ✐

Well.
Off to a great start. 〰

The Return of Hall Shark

At my locker,
someone grabs
my towel off from behind.
"Hey!"

When did the "E"
on Claire's compass
start to stand for
"Enraged"?

"Nick texted me," she says.
"He thinks there's something
wrong with you, and I'm, like,
where should I start?"

No matter what he told her,
no matter what she knows,
it's okay. It's fine. Play it cool.

"I'm sorry he's hurt, but
he's better off. Believe me."

She twists the towel into a rope.
I take a few steps back, in case
she's planning strangulation.
"Addie, you lied to him! He feels awful
that you didn't trust him enough to tell him
you quit the team."

"Know why I lied? I didn't want him
looking at me the way you are! Like I'm a
huge disappointment!"

And the Oscar for playing it cool goes to . . .

"Nick cares about you. I do, too.
And we thought we knew
what you cared about, but apparently
we have no idea."

She drops the towel.
Walks away.

WWMD?

She would go to her next class.

She would let Emily borrow her notes.

She would copy down logarithms.

She would complete all the problems plus
the extra credit.

She would start on homework for tomorrow.

She would try not to think about it.

Try not to think about it.

Try not to think.

Reduced to a Womb

Maybe Mary loved to run
or fish or swim or play
poker.

Maybe she hated figs
and once lobbed one at
the rabbi's son.

Maybe she hitched up her skirt
in the stream, let minnows kiss
her curious knees.

Maybe she had a favorite song,
a dimple on her chin, a secret dream
that, after a while, not even she
remembered. ⪜

Super Virgin

It's a bird! It's a plane!
It's Juliana flapping back
from the bathroom
wearing my towel for a cape.

"Watch me leap tall
penises in a single bound!"

"Leaping Tall Penises. My new
band name."

"There you go." From behind
my chair she grabs my shoulders,
starts to massage. "Show Nick the Dick
who the real rock star is."

"I don't know, Juliana. I'm starting to think
I overreacted."

"Well, so what if you did?
Nick sounds like a pretty good guy.
Pope Francis is a good guy, too.
That doesn't mean you have to
go out with him."

"True." I let myself sink into
her healing hands.

"And to think I'm not even a virgin,
I just play one on TV."

An Annoying Little Boy

keeps rolling his toy car under our table.
"Stop it, Jeremy," says his babysitter.
"Stop it right now." But Jeremy
doesn't stop it. After the fifth time,
she snatches the car, shoves it in her purse.
Jeremy screams like he's been stabbed.
Kicks. Knocks over his juice. Pretty soon
the babysitter looks like she wants to
shove Jeremy in her purse and crawl in
after him.

Super Virgin swoops over,
uses her cape to help wipe up the mess,
and returns with a soggy wad
she tells me she'll take home and wash
and give back to me tomorrow.
I'm about to tell her that's okay,
she doesn't have to.
Then I picture my towel
communing with her dirty
laundry—T-shirts, jeans, socks,
underwear,
and I say, "Sure. Whenever. No rush."

Speaking of Tomorrow . . .

"Let's meet somewhere else,"
Juliana suggests.

"Don't you have a . . ."
shrink appointment? "I mean,
where would we meet?"

"I was thinking the lake."

Oh, hell no. "Nice try.
I'm not putting myself through
that again."

"What do you mean? We ran there
together once. It was fun."

"Fun? Ha! You ran backward half the time,
you big show-off."

She laughs. "I was being nice!
I was waiting for you to catch up!"

"Yeah, well clearly now I'd be the one
running backward since you are
old and decrepit, and I am
a youthful gazelle who is way too
nice to want to put *you* through that."

"Look, who says we have to run? We can walk. Bike. Rollerblade. Skip and sing 'Jingle Bells.' Whatever you want."

Whatever I want? Hmmmmm . . .

"Okay, fine. See you there."

Double Uh-oh

At 3:14, while I am supposed to
be at practice Mom texts me
to *Come home now.*

I text back *On my way*

before I remember
I'm still supposed to be
practicing.

Peppermint Tea

Mom stirs and stirs
long after the sugar
has dissolved.

Can't she understand?
"I didn't want to disappoint you."
Again. As usual.

"Here's what disappoints me.
That you would lie to us
about something so trivial."

"Thanks a lot. Thanks for
calling the sport I've devoted
my entire stupid life to trivial."

This is Nick's fault.
Correction: Nick the Dick.
He showed up
at her library
to tell her he's "concerned."

"Honey, all I'm saying is,
compared to what we went through
a few months ago, this seems
like nothing at all."

She takes a sip that by now must be
ice-cold.

My Dad Can Fix Anything, Part II

And if he can't, his friend Ron at work
knows a great sports medicine guy.

"Wouldn't hurt to get you checked out."

"She's fine, Steve," Mom says.
"Physically."

"What about those side aches?
She never had those before."

He doesn't say "before" what.
Won't say it. Can't.

"I didn't have any side aches.
I just . . . I couldn't . . . I'm
really sorry, okay?"

"We're not angry," he is quick
to assure me. "We just want you to be . . ."

Good?
Normal?
Not a colossal pain in the ass?

"Happy."

Hurricane Season

On my way upstairs,

I knock the photo

behind the piano

like it's nothing.

Nothing at all.

Mary's Parents

Sure, they tried their best
not to treat her any different.

What choice did they have?

After all, she was still their daughter,
and they had promised
God to love her no matter what
crazy shit her body could do.

Nick Texts

DO YOU HATE ME?
I wouldn't say I'm your biggest fan
YOU GAVE ME NO CHOICE
Stop shouting
????
You're hurting my ears
Your behavior required intervention
I didn't do anything
My point exactly. You don't DO anything. Except maybe run away.
Leave me alone
I will. Once I make sure you're okay
You know what would make me okay?
What?
IF EVERYONE WOULD STOP ASKING ME IF I'M OKAY
Forget it. Forget I even tried

Possible Morality Project #2

Jesus: Savior or Busybody?
by Adrienne Solokowski

Jesus ran around performing miracles. Feeding the hungry.
Curing the sick. Raising the dead. But did any of those
people even <u>ask</u> for his help?

Take his first miracle. He and Mary were at a wedding,
and he changed water into wine. Really considerate, right?
Except maybe the bride and groom were relieved to run out
of alcohol because their guests were already pretty turnt.
So then they're all, thanks a lot, Jesus, now the party can
get even more out of control.

And, okay, it seems from the Bible like most of the lepers
<u>wanted</u> to be cured. But what if afterward they realized
how much more peaceful it was being shunned? Nobody
following them around telling them how lucky they must
feel, blah, blah, blah.

Then there's Lazarus. When he was sick, his sisters Mary
and Martha sent a message to Jesus asking him to come
help, but Jesus waited <u>two whole days.</u> He didn't show
up until he knew Lazarus was already dead, and then he
has the nerve to be mad! He's pissed at Mary and Martha

for being all. Why weren't you here earlier? He brings Lazarus back to life knowing full well that Lazarus was in heaven. Heaven! Sorry, no more eternal bliss for you, L, you have to return to your hovel in the desert so Jesus can show off!

As Jesus was carrying his cross up the hill to the place where he would be crucified, a woman named Veronica stepped from the jeering crowd of spectators and wiped the sweat and blood from his face. How did he thank her? With candy? Flowers? Nope. He left an image of his face on the cloth. Like he was Justin Bieber. ⚡

Um, Yeah

Possibly
not.

Thursday: Crusader Day

1, 2, 3, 4, we've got spirit,
you need more!

I'm on the bleachers in the gym
suffering through the mandatory pep rally
when someone taps me on the back.
Iris. "Craig told me about you and Nick.
So sad."

5, 6, 7, 8, we've got spirit,
we are great!

"It's not that sad. But thanks."

7, 8, 9, 10, we've got spirit,
we'll say it again!

"To be honest? I wasn't
surprised. Nick is such a slut."

"Say that again?"

1, 2, 3, 4 . . .

As the Cheer Squad Begins

to slaughter a Katy Perry routine
Iris explains, "Well, you know. He stole you
from Craig. Though obviously I'm glad
he did! Still. What a shitty thing to do
to his best friend, right?"

"He . . ." Talk about
revisionist history.
So the real thief
wants me to believe
that St. Craig stood piously by
while Nick dragged me off
by my hair? "He didn't
steal me."

"WHAT?" She leans in, trying to hear
over the roar of "Roar."

"HE DIDN'T STEAL ME!"

"OKAY. WHATEVER." The pyramid
wobbles. The music ends. And then, "Craig's
always telling me that Nick is a great guy, but I think
he's kind of a jerk."

"Hey, Aren't You Supposed to Be Down There?"

She means standing with the team
while Karla Davies, head of cheer squad,
hands Coach the mic so he can remind us
to come to the meet tomorrow
and support these little ladies—did Claire's
eyes just roll out of her head?—who have
been working darn hard and gotten off
the season to a heck of a start.

"I quit cross country."

"Oh," says Iris. Her interest in sports
stops at channel surfing. "God. This thing
is never going to end."

Seems that way.

Lay Teachers

They aren't priests or nuns,
so, technically, they can get laid.
How's that for an un-fun fact?
Especially when applied to
lay history teacher Ms. Tran,
who is married to lay math teacher
Coach.

The picture on Ms. Tran's desk
from their honeymoon is enough to make
a girl regret taking American Civ
so soon after lunch.

Sometimes when he sees her in the hall
he blows a kiss.

Sometimes he lingers in her doorway
until the bell rings,
and I have to squeeze past him,
or do I?

Muscle Memory ✑

The more you run
away,
the more natural it feels.

You can speed right by
the classroom
like it's not even there;

you can find yourself
in your car
in the parking lot at the lake

before your brain
can form objections,

before your lungs
finally remember
how to breathe. 〰

Feral

Here I am, escaped
from captivity, out in the wild.
What if I just never go back?

I could
live here at the lake,
burrow under the bandshell,
menace picnics,
scrounge potato salad,
suck the marrow from
Popsicle sticks,
scent mark the monkey bars.

I would
be a playground rumor,
an area legend
lumbering from the woods
one summer night at dusk
to King Kong climb the lifeguard stand
and howl down at the huddled families, the terrified couples,
the Animal Control officer with the tranquilizer gun.

In the Meantime . . .

How can I kill
an hour
until Juliana gets here?

Skipping Around the Lake

Two little girls being pulled in a wagon
point at me and giggle.

Grumpy ducks scatter from my path.

Some dude on a bike yells, "Yeah, baby,
love that bounce!"

An old woman walking a beagle
scowls, jerks the leash in tight—

That's right, ma'am,
don't let Snoopy get too close.
Clearly I'm completely
high.

From a Distance

I'm not sure.
Wait. No.
Yes. Definitely.
Her
jogging toward
me.

Her hair
her face
her arms
her face
her legs
her face
her boobs
her face
her lips . . .
Definitely
her lips
close enough
now
to
kiss.

Variations on a Theme

Did that just happen?

That did *not* just happen.

Let's just pretend that didn't happen.

"Wow," Juliana says,
a little flushed,
a little out of breath.
"What was that?"

The Swimming Beach

Ask me how I got here
and I'll say I must have
levitated.

The sun dips behind a cloud.
I'm shivering from
the heat of her shoulder
almost touching mine.

Any second now
she'll take off toward the water.
I'll watch her disappear
with one flip of her shimmery tail.

How did I get here?
The only possible explanation is . . .

"I'm Such an Idiot."

"You're not an idiot."

I scrape at the sand, clawing out
a hole big enough to swallow my fist.
Or my heart. (It's basic anatomy—
either would fit.)

"No, I *am*. I don't know
what's wrong with me.
First Craig. Then Nick.
And now . . . I just kind of fall
into these relationships. . . ."

I start to get up, but she
presses her hand against my leg—
Her. Hand. Against. My.
Stop.

"Okay, first of all?" she says.
"I'm not a ditch. Or a canyon. You
didn't fall into me. I'm your friend."

And Second of All?

"I want to show you something.
It's the reason why I'm seeing a shrink.
Ready?"

She's pushes up her sweatshirt sleeves,
holds out her pale arms, twists her pale
wrists toward the fading light.

Oh God, I knew it,
The Scars. The scars. The scars are
not there?

Fruit Salad

Monday mango, Tuesday kiwi, Wednesday
Georgia peach—her roommate Heather
had a different scented lotion for every
day of the week, and Juliana says they smelled
revolting splattered all over the dorm room floor.

She can joke about it now. "It was like
I'd actually died, and hell was
a Bath & Body Works. I'm just glad I stopped
before Thursday." She makes a face. "Coconut."

Not that she'd planned to stop.
Not that she didn't wait for a night
when Heather was out,
didn't lie curled in a ball on her bed
clutching the blade until she finally slashed
three plastic tubes.

"I was so angry. So disgusted with myself
for not being able to go through with it."

"So you took it out on the moisturizer?"

Perfect, Addie. Gold star for sensitivity.

But—cue big sigh of relief—she halfway
laughs. "How dare it make my skin
so silky smooth!"

The Less Hilarious Part

was having to move back home
and take Incompletes in all her classes
and try out two different shrinks,
and try out three different meds
until she found ones that didn't
give her the spins.

"Oh, and Heather won't
talk to me anymore."

"Heather's loss."

"I don't blame her. She thought
she knew me. Then she found out
she really didn't."

This Is the Part

where I tell her
my secret,
right?

WRONG
WRONG
WRONG
WRONG
WRONG
WRONG
WRONG

This Is the Part

Where I turn into Nick
or Claire
or my parents
and ask, "But you're okay
now?"

Where she turns into me
and answers, "You don't
have to worry."

Where me-as-Nick-or-Claire-or-my-parents
feels relieved.

Where me-as-me wonders,
is she just saying that
because she knows I need it
to be true?

From the Department of Obvious Metaphors

We're walking to the parking lot.
I start to cross the bike path
when Juliana shrieks and yanks me back.

"Holy shit," I say. "Where did
that asshole come from?"

"I don't know, but he's going
hella fast. You could have gotten
really hurt."

So when we get to my car
and start to lean into a kiss, I
I force myself to
put on the brakes at a hug.

Dinner Alone

Mom and Dad are out
at the church's fall gala.
A note directs me to leftovers,
but I go for cereal instead,
carry my bowl to the couch,
start flipping channels.

CSI?
Pet Weddings?
Dancing with Hoarders?
Doctor Who?

Then there's
The Juliana Show.

When I finally
open my eyes,
slide my fingers
out of my pants,
my Cheerios are mush,
and I am somehow watching
golf?

At the Last Supper

In the moment
right after
Jesus told his disciples,
"Take and eat, this is
my body,"
did he worry at all
they might say, "No,
thanks, we had a
big lunch?"

It was a risk,
offering himself
to his friends.
Luckily, they were
hungry.
Or at least
they took a few bites
just to be polite.

Mom vs. Hurricane

It's back!
Hanging on the wall
in a brand-new silver frame,

daring me
on my way upstairs
to do my worst.

I touch the glass,
leave a streaky print . . .

Hurricane Addie
has done enough
damage.

Nick Texts

Hey
Hey
Still mad?
Enraged
Okay . . .
Kidding
For real?
Not kidding about the kidding ☺
So did you hear about Milo and Sabrina?
????
Back together
No!
Bye-bye bitch queen sea life
Hello wanting to die inside her smile
😛
Hey, that song was sweet
Yep. That's why I asked him
To marry you?
Ha. Promise not to judge?
Swear
I asked him to write my lyrics
Brave
They turned out okay
He's done? Mr. Speedy
Dude is powered by luuuuuvvvvvvvvvvvvvvvv

How emo is it?
It's called "Boner Motel"
Bet that rocks pretty hard
For real!
Can't wait to hear
Come to the Halloween show at Arthur's?

Who Knows

I just might
go to that show.

I just might
bring a friend.

WWND?

if he knew
about me
and Juliana,
about what we
were up to
this afternoon?

Probably
FREAK
THE
FUCK
OUT
and then, hopefully,
be cool.

Friday: Canned Food Drive Day

when we answer Christ's call
to "feed my sheep"
with creamed corn and wax beans.

During morning announcements,
a quick reminder
for teachers to please excuse
the cross country team—
Go, Crusaders!—for their meet
against Bloomington.

Can't catch Claire's eye.
Finally I sneak her a text:
GOOD LUCK!!!!!!!!!!!!!!!

Ten minutes later . . .

Fifteen minutes later . . .

Two hours later . . .

No answer.

Hall Shark: The Next Generation

A real great white
would have starved by now.

My prey slips away
in the library,
the third-floor bathroom,
the junior lounge
where useless Meredith
has no clue: "I think Claire's
in art. No, wait, chemistry?"

At the food drive donation table

I come close,

then closer.

I'm ready to strike . . .

So what should I say?

By the time I figure that out
she's gone
without a trace
except for
two family-sized jars of Ragú.

The Church Responds

to women who've had abortions
with compassion.

It says so right here
in our textbooks, page fifty-three.

Allison agrees. "Hope's Journey
is all about compassion."

"Tell us how they express it,"
says Sister Barbara, as if Allison
needs the encouragement.

"They have this whole process
that helps a woman let go of her guilt.
And it's not the same for
everyone. Like, some women write
letters to their babies. Or songs or poems.
Or hold a little funeral. Or plant a tree
or buy a locket to remember."

I've lost control of my hand, it shoots
into the air. "Trees and jewelry are nice
and all, but how is that letting go?"

Sister Barbara lets Allison answer. "Well,
it's ritual. They can't heal unless they
acknowledge what they did instead of
running away from it."

Really? "That doesn't sound like healing to me. That sounds like, I don't know, gouging out the wound."

"Exactly!" Allison chirps. "They have to *feel* the pain to release it."

"What a load of . . ."

"Respectful tones, please, ladies. Okay, I'd like you to spend these last ten minutes of class journaling about what compassion means to you."

I don't believe... ~~

I can't figure out...

This stupid class...

Morality = More Bullshit...

I'm not sure what...

What I'm trying to say...

How can anyone possibly...

Does she really think...

Dear ?????????????????????

Dear What...

Dear Who... ≋

Dear You, ✎

She wants me to believe
you are up there
checking your celestial in-box
for my apology.

They want me to imagine you
as a person,
not a permanent blank—

a girl with Nick's smile,
a boy with my eyes,
a baby
with my father's hair,
my mother's chin,
my grandmother's crazy long toes.

Whatever you would have looked like,
whoever you might have been,
I have no way of knowing.

All I know for sure
is I would never want you
to hate yourself.

I would love you
enough to never make you
write a stupid fucking letter
like this one.

Love,
Me ⟆

What I Really Need to Say Is

"I'm sorry
I was such an asshole. There.
Now will you stop avoiding me?"

"I'm not avoiding you, dummy."
Claire's kneeling by her locker
surrounded by her uniform:
socks, shorts, sweats. She looks
like she's rising up from a puddle
of melted candy canes. "I just . . ." She
shakes her head. "I have to go."

"Well, good luck, okay? Not
that you'll need it."

She stops cramming shit in her duffel.
"Are you fucking kidding me?"

Sick of talking
to the top of her head,
I plop down beside her.
"What?"

"You're right.
I don't need luck.
I need a miracle.
Or a lobotomy.
Or a . . ."
She flings out her arms,

almost whacking a passing freshman.
"A time machine. To go back to
when you weren't a quitter,
and I ran my personal best
every meet because
you were there to pace me."

So Claire's not completely selfless.
That's a relief.

"Bloomington's course is flat.
You'll PR. No problem."

"Ha. Easy for you to say."

We sit silently surrounded by
her mess until she says, "Can you at least
lend me your water bottle?
Mine leaks."

Of Course I'm Not Jealous

Scruffy dude—Juliana says
his name is Seth—starts
to make my usual.
Except today I want two.
To go.

"This one for your friend?
She's gonna be psyched.
We got hazelnut syrup
back in."

So what if he knows
what she likes. So what.
Right?

After the shrink, she gets in my car,
takes a long slow sip. "Mmmmm.
Yummy."

Watch your back, Seth.

Almost There

She's not going to make it.
We should have stood farther in.
No.
This is where she needs us.
For the kick.

Juliana points. "Here they come."

Two Bloomington runners
shoot out from the trees.
I concentrate on the space
behind them, willing Claire to fill it.
Come on, come on, come on . . .
There!

She's gaining.
No, she's fading.

"Pick it up, Claire!" shouts Juliana.
"Finish strong!"

My sign doesn't say

MISFORTUNE COOKIE

or

YOUR ELEGANT PANIC

or

FEEL THE CHEESY BREAD

I'm not here to be cute.

I'm here to run
alongside her,
here to show her
she is

ALMOST THERE.

Post-race Analysis

You didn't have to do that.

Hey, you don't get to be Bo Peep's only
lost sheep.

Can you believe Bo Peep's sad little goatee?
Like he skinned the sex caterpillar for a rug.

Before it had the chance to grow into
a beautiful sex butterfly.

Thanks for ruining nature for me.

Seriously, Addie. What was I
supposed to say when he asked me
how my season was going?
I can't pretend to be some superstar
college athlete just so he can list me
under "achievements" on his resume.

Speaking of achievements, do you remember
your PR for this course?

Duh.

What was it?

What was yours, hotshot?

Race me to the car. If you beat me,
I'll tell you.

In that case, prepare to
confess!

The Assumption of the Virgin Mary

When her days on Earth were over
God lifted her gently into heaven
body and soul.

Rising into the light
she must have felt
the way I feel now
in the middle of this miracle
with Juliana
leaning close
to whisper her time in my ear.

Sunday Morning

At Java Joe's.
I'm going to be here
awhile,

so I
treat myself to a cinnamon bagel,
smile at the woman grading papers,
make a silly face for the squawking twins,
head back to my favorite table,
arrange my "office"—laptop, notebook, pen.
Check the door. Check it again.
Picture her coming through it.
Picture me standing up.
Picture her coming closer . . .

Stop that, Addie.
Get to work.

Due Monday

Sister Barbara said pick a topic
I'm passionate about.

I've got nothin'
on social justice,
euthanasia,
animal rights,
fracking.

All I've got
are my poems.

Easy enough
to type them up.
Not so easy
to turn them in.

What the Hell

Sister Barbara wants passion?

Here it comes!

"Earth to Addie."

When I look up,
she lifts the towel off her shoulders,
lays it on mine. "Fresh and clean, like
I promised. Though not fluffed and folded.
Sorry."

It's warm.
It smells like her.
Yum.

"Why so intense?" she asks. "What
are you working on?"

I practice handing them over.

She Closes My Notebook

Opens her mouth.
Closes it.
Opens it and says,
"So this is your story?"

At the bottom of a big hill,
you always have a choice:
Do you keep going
or do you quit?

This time I decide
to keep going,
to open my mouth,
to tell her
everything.

Acknowledgments

So many people were important to me during the writing of this book. You know who you are, or, if you don't, please see me after class. A few of you earned extra credit: Tina Wexler, Martha Mihalick, and Ron Koertge. There aren't enough gold stars in the universe to express how much you helped.

No one ever has to face an unplanned pregnancy alone.
Organizations exist at the community and national level that
teens can turn to for help. Here are a few online resources.

Planned Parenthood https://www.plannedparenthood.org/teens

Abortion Care Network https://www.abortioncarenetwork.org/

Backline http://yourbackline.org/

National Network of Abortion Funds
http://www.fundabortionnow.org/

Abortion Conversation Project
http://www.abortionconversationproject.org/

Catholics for Choice http://catholicsforchoice.org/